バイリンガル俳句集
A Collection of Bilingual Haiku

新 編
星の雫
STARDROPS
Revisited

青山夕璃
Yuri Aoyama

七月堂

Stardrops

Revisited

A Collection of Bilingual Haiku

© 2017 by Yuri Aoyama

First Edition ISBN978-4-87944-274-1 C0092

Publisher: Shichigatsudo Ltd

2-26-6-103 Matsubara, Setagaya, Tokyo 156-0043 Japan

Tel: +81-3-3325-5717   Fax: +81-3-3325-5731

Email: July@shichigatsudo.co.jp

目次
CONTENTS

冬星座

Winter Constellations

5

星祭

The Star Festival

49

流星

Shooting Stars

83

後記

Acknowledgements

冬星座

Winter Constellations

長編に泣き短編に笑ふ秋

（第 18 回国際俳句交流協会 [HIA] 俳句大会　特選）

crying over long stories
laughing over short stories
autumn

(The Tokusen Prize in the 18th Haiku International Association
[HIA] Haiku Contest)

秋の水静かに父の老ゆるかな

（第 35 回時雨忌全国俳句大会　特選）

autumn water

my father is gradually growing

older

(The Tokusen Prize in the 35th Shigureki Nationwide Haiku
Contest)

長月や暑き東京寒きパリ

September —
Tokyo is hot
Paris is cold

8　—冬星座

風を聞きパリの落葉の降りしきる

hearing the wind
autumn leaves in Paris
fall thickly

霧深きロンドン塔の音なき夜

with dense fog
a soundless night
at the Tower of London

帰国して紅葉美し人優し

back from abroad

autumnal tints are lovely

people are friendly

旅人の旅びと想ふ初時雨

travellers

think about travellers

the first rain of winter

白鳥や波なき湖の青きこと

white swans —
how blue the lake
with no waves !

黄昏の色と思へば紅葉濃く

imagining autumnal tints
as the colour of dusk
they look deeper

別れ霜鬼女伝説の里の夜に

late spring frosts
on a night in the village
of the she-devil legend

冬の蝶恋の泪にあるわけは

a winter butterfly

the reason for

tears of love is

異国めく京の街角クリスマス

street corners in Kyoto
turning exotic
Christmas

冬星座友に未完の詩集あり

winter constellations
my friend's poetry book
remains unpublished

風花や名声といふ名の孤独

light snowflakes
from a clear sky —
the solitude named fame

霙 降る彼にわたしに元カレに

sleet falls
on my boyfriend and me
on my ex-boyfriend

鏡中に雪女の影音もなく

in the mirror
the shadow of a snow woman
with no sound

今はもう君の声なき雪の街

now

your voice is no longer heard

a snowy town

雪月夜出会ひと別れ重ねつつ

a moonlit night after snowfall
I recall repeated meetings and
partings

早梅やひつそり紅に白に咲き

early plum blossoms —
silently blooming in crimson
blooming in white

朝影に透け梅の紅梅の白

clarified in the morning sun

crimson of plum blossoms

white of plum blossoms

被災者を見守りくるる春の星

（第 31 回世田谷文学賞　秀作）

watching over

disaster victims

spring stars

(The Shusaku Prize in the 31st Setagaya
Literary Awards)

水仙や復興の風吹き初むる

（第 31 回世田谷文学賞　秀作）

narcissuses —
the wind of rebuilding
starts blowing

(The Shusaku Prize in the 31st Setagaya
Literary Awards)

水温むショパン弾く指なめらかに

water warms up
fingers playing Chopin
are smooth

生きるもの死にゆくものに春の月

to the living
to the dying
spring moon

子猫来て相席ねだるカフェテラス

a kitten
comes and pesters to share the table
a café terrace

白椿夕日の色を重ねけり

**white camellias
the colour of the evening sun
is added**

亀鳴くや花嫁が元男とは

turtles crying —
the bride used to be
a man

恋猫のあるじ同志も恋ほのか

owners too

of cats in love

are faintly in love

モルディブへ続く航路や風光る

a sea route
to the Maldives —
a shining spring breeze

ペアグラスしっとり包む春の闇

falling on
two glasses in a gentle mood
spring darkness

主役あり脇役もあり石鹸玉

the starring role exists

supporting roles too exist

soap bubbles

リラの香か今別れゆく人の香か

the scent of lilacs?
the scent of a person
leaving me?

高き山低き山あり遅桜

high mountains and
low mountains rise
late cherry blossoms

花の上花の下にも花の精

above cherry blossoms
under cherry blossoms too
floral fairies

花散るやひとひらの詩の生まれきて

cherry blossoms scattering —
a piece of a poem
being born

花吹雪悲報吉報包み込み

storms of
falling cherry blossoms covering up
bad and good news

落花して花柄となるベレー帽

cherry blossoms falling
a floral pattern is added to
a beret

風すれ違ひ花吹雪すれ違ひ

the winds passing each other
storms of falling cherry blossoms
passing each other

梵鐘にふと散りなづむ夕桜

the bell of a Buddhist temple
evening cherry blossoms linger before falling
for a moment

われの手にわれの心に飛花落花

to my hand

to my mind

cherry blossoms fly and fall

花の過去花の未来を想ふ夜

the night thinking about
the past of cherry blossoms
the future of cherry blossoms

日の桜宵の桜やひとり旅

cherry blossoms in the day
cherry blossoms in the evening —
a solitary journey

星祭

The Star Festival

遠ざかるロンドンの薔薇街の音

roses in London and
the sounds of the town
disappear from sight

水中花喜んでをり泣いてをり

suichuka
rejoicing
crying

---

suichuka : an artificial flower which "blooms" when immersed
in water

一輪の薔薇ひそと咲き一景に

a single rose

secretly coming out to become

a part of a scene

追憶といふ薔薇からの贈りもの

a gift
named reminiscence
from roses

鈴蘭の白より白き香りなし

no other white scent
than the white colour
of a lily-of-the-valley

蛍火や風に現はれ風に消え

firefly lights —
appearing in the wind
disappearing in the wind

夜会服くちなしの香の白を添へ

an evening dress
the white of the scent of gardenias
is added

一重帯ときて絡まる恋いろいろ

undoing

a single summer *obi*

various loves are involved

---

obi : a sash worn with a kimono

薫風に瑠璃のさざめくエーゲ海

an early summer breeze
blue colour ruffles
on the Aegean Sea

白夜とはいとかぐはしくうとましく

a white night
is so pleasant
so repugnant

子の匂ひ波の匂ひや夏休

the smell of children
the smell of waves —
summer vacation

少年に恋の兆しや星祭

to a boy

the sign of love —

the Star Festival

---

the Star Festival : a festival celebrating a Chinese legend and held on the night of 7th July, when slips of coloured paper with prayers written on them are attached to branches of bamboo trees.

これは恋あれは友情髪洗ふ

this is love
that is friendship
washing my hair

悲恋とは開かぬ百合のつぼみにも

a tragic love
existing even in an unopened bud
of a lily

虹立つや父の俳句と母の詩と

a rainbow appears —
my father's haiku and
my mother's poem

睡蓮や水に言葉を置くやうに

**water lilies —
like putting words
on the water**

香水や淡き秘め事振りかへり

perfume —
thinking back to
a faint love affair

言へぬ恋言はぬ恋あり遠花火

love I cannot say

love I would not say

distant fireworks

風蘭や夢はガラスのごときもの

**Japanese wind orchids —
a dream is something like
glass**

バレリーナの君軽やかに爽やかに

as a ballerina

you dance lightly and

delightfully

夜露にはＪＡＺＺの香りがよく似合ふ

for night dew

the scent of jazz is

well-matched

夜の秋シャガールは青澄みわたり

**cool late summer night
Chagall's blue becoming
perfectly clear**

ヴィオロンの音色変はりて窓の秋

the tone
of a violin has changed
autumn windows

秋風の吹く青春の一ページ

**autumn wind
blows on one page
of my youth**

秋の蝶恋捜しゆきさがしゆき

an autumn butterfly
looking for
looking for love

秋の夜のことのひとつに恋煩ひ

one of the things
on an autumn night
lovesickness

チェロの音に闇の濃くなる秋の暮

with the sound of a cello
the darkness grows deeper
autumn dusk

十三夜恋とは知らず別れけり

on the thirteenth night
I left you without noticing
it was love

わが思春期は

どんぐりや母は仲良し父は憂し

my adolescence

acorns —
my mother is compatible
my father is incompatible

花野来て花野を帰る鳥の影

coming to a field of autumn wildflowers

returning from a field of autumn wildflowers

the shadows of birds

星なきに街は木犀の香に眠る

beneath no stars

a town sleeps in the scent of

sweet olives

月去りて月恋ふ影やかぐや姫

the moon leaving

the shadow longing for it —

Kaguyahime

Kaguyahime : the Shining Princess (in the early Heian period Tale of the Bamboo Cutter); a bamboo cutter finds a baby princess who has come from the moon inside a piece of shining bamboo. Calling her Kaguyahime, he and his wife bring her up as their daughter, but she eventually returns to the moon.

コスモスの影にも風の吹く日かな

a day when
the wind blows on the shadows too
of cosmos

流星

Shooting Stars

消えし街消えし人影原爆忌

（第７回鈴木しづ子顕彰会いのちの俳句大会　特選）

vanished towns

vanished human figures

the atomic bomb anniversary

(The Tokusen Prize in the 7th Suzuki Shizuko Kenshokai
Inochi no Haiku Contest)

目に沁みる百合の白さや爆心地

white of lilies

hurting the eyes —

the centre of a bomb blast

影たちの声なき声や広島忌

shadows'
voiceless voices —
the Hiroshima atomic bomb anniversary

夕凪や被爆二世の声高く

evening calm of the sea —
the second-generation of atomic bomb survivors
whose voices are strong

終戦日記憶は波へ波へ消え

（第8回鈴木しづ子顕彰会いのちの俳句大会　秀逸賞）

the anniversary of the war's end

memories fade away into waves

into waves

(The Shuitsu Prize in the 8th Suzuki Shizuko Kenshokai
Inochi no Haiku Contest)

戦死した夫に恋文冬すみれ

love letters
to my husband killed during the war
winter violets

曼珠沙華母の語りし大空襲

red spider lilies
my mother talked about
the major air raid

戦跡に夏菊の影父の影

in an old battlefield
the shadows of summer chrysanthemums
the shadow of my father

生者死者祈りはひとつ原爆忌

（第 53 回俳人協会全国俳句大会　入選）

the living and the dead

are united in one prayer

the atomic bomb anniversary

(The Nyusen Prize in the 53rd Association of Haiku Poets
Nationwide Haiku Contest)

終戦日生者の誓ひ海を越え

the anniversary of the war's end
the vows of the living
crossing the sea

タヒチ着水平線に星流れ

arriving in Tahiti
a shooting star falling
to the horizon

秋の声星の雫の影白く

a hint of autumn
the shadows of stardrops
are white

ニューカレドニアの星空の下で

夏潮やサザンクロスを捜せずに

beneath a starry sky in New Caledonia

the summer tide —
I still cannot find
the Southern Cross

星涼しサンテグジュペリ読み終へて

cool stars
after I have read a book by
Saint-Exupéry

モルディブの潮の香強き星月夜

the smell of the tide
in the Maldives is strong
a bright starry night

人影も波もなき夜の天の川

on a night
with no human figures or waves
the Milky Way

カリブの眠れぬ夜に

波と来て波と去りゆく星月夜

on a sleepless night in the Caribbean

coming with waves

leaving with waves

a bright starry night

星飛びし北回帰線君の声

**a shooting star
on the Tropic of Cancer
your voice**

道迷ふ銀河の旅に出たものの

missing my way
though I go on a journey
to the galaxy

銀河抜け銀河ぬけ君棲む惑星へ

going through the galaxy
going through the galaxy
to the planet where you live

流星は星の王子の豪速球

a shooting star is

the Little Prince's

overpowering fastball

星に問ひ星と語りて帰り花

asking stars
talking with stars
reflowering

行秋や星の韻文降る小道

autumn passes —
starry verses fall on
a path

淡き日に淡き影伸び冬薔薇(ふゆさうび)

（第17回常陸国小野小町文芸賞　秀逸賞）

in the faint sunlight

faint shadows are cast

winter roses

(The Shuitsu Prize in the 17th Hitachi no Kuni
Ono no Komachi Literary Awards)

後記

　幼い頃から星を眺めるのが好きで流れ星を数えな
がら大きくなりました。地上には戦争や核の脅威な
どがいまだに溢れていますが、天上の星たちは絶え
ることなく希望の光を放ち私たちを暖かく見守って
くれています。戦後生まれの私がそんな星たちへ感
謝を捧げ平和への願いを込めて綴った祈りの数々が
流星になって皆様のお手元に届くように願っており
ます。

　今回は国際俳句交流協会の会員として出版させて
いただきました。俳句の英訳に関しては様々な考え
方や方法があると思いますが、拙訳はイギリス英語
による単なる一例として読者の皆様に受け取ってい
ただけたら大変幸いです。

　最後に、拙俳句へ様々なご意見をくださった方々
と出版に関していろいろなご提案をしていただいた
七月堂の知念明子氏へ感謝を表します。また、英訳
に関して貴重なアドバイスをしていただいた上智大
学名誉教授 Peter Milward 先生、早稲田大学教授
Adrian Pinnington 先生へ心より感謝を表し筆をおき
ます。

2017 年 1 月 12 日
青山夕璃

Acknowledgements

Since I was little, I have been fond of watching stars and have grown up counting shooting stars. Though the world is filled with wars and nuclear threats, etc. still now, stars in the sky are endlessly generating lights of hope watching over us warmly. As someone born after the war, I hope that my various prayers that I composed with gratitude to such stars and with a wish for peace transform into shooting stars and reach all of you.

This time I independently published this book as a member of The Haiku International Association. Considering that there can be various ways of thinking and methods for translating haiku, I hope that every reader will regard my translations simply as part of an experiment in British English.

Finally, I would like to thank those who gave me valuable comments on my haiku and Ms Akiko Chinen of Shichigatsudo Ltd for various assistance in publishing my book. Also, I would like to thank from the bottom of my heart Dr Peter Milward, Professor Emeritus at Sophia University and Dr Adrian Pinnington, Professor at Waseda University who both gave me valuable advice when I was translating my haiku into English.

12th January, 2017
Yuri Aoyama

著者略歴

青山夕璃（あおやま・ゆり）

東京都生まれ

著作　2006 年
　　　　詩集『風のアルビオン』（土曜美術社出版販売）
　　　　2009 年
　　　　バイリンガル俳句集『星の雫』（七月堂）

訳書　2011 年
　　　　響音遊戯シリーズ 7『GIRL FRIEND』（七月堂）

所属　ザ・ポエトリー・ソサエティ (London, U.K.)
　　　　国際俳句交流協会 (Tokyo, Japan)

The author :

Yuri Aoyama was born in Tokyo and published her first poetry book, *Albion of the Wind* in 2006 and her first haiku book, *Stardrops* in 2009 in Japan. Also, she translated Japanese poems into English in the English poetry book entitled *GIRL FRIEND* published by Shichigatsudo. She is a member of The Poetry Society in London, U.K. and The Haiku International Association in Tokyo, Japan.

新編　星の雫

発行日・2017 年 1 月 12 日
著　者・青山夕璃
発行者・知念明子
発行所・七月堂
　東京都世田谷区松原 2-26-6-103
　電話 03(3325)5717
　ＦＡＸ　03(3325)5731

© Yuri Aoyama 2017, Printed in Japan
ISBN978-4-87944-274-1 C0092
落丁・乱丁本はお取り替えいたします。